THE STORIES WHICH ARE ABOUT TO COME

ALL ARE REGISTERED

YOGENDRA NIKALE

Contents

ONE

x frenchise

hardcore criminals from various countries are escaped from the prison and have been seen in miami. and mr. gibbons sents his agent to uncover the mystery but the criminals kills the agent and makes it look like an accident. and mr. gibbons needs a agent just to know whats the plan of the criminals but he didnt bother to involve the old xxx team and even their cover is also blown. he wanted someone new but a stronger one. mr. gibbons always has in mind a guy who is in mental assylum.

a guy named max is in assylum, he beats his opponent on the same date every year. no matter where his enemy is. max breaks every security and every lock to beat him. and the day comes and mr. gibbons knew he wont work on the date which max wants his revenge. so mr. gibbons waits for max to get released. there are people who are helping max to escape, the people who made a deal with him. max helped those people and in return they have to help him escape from any country and cage. and the helpers also provide the address of his enemy.

max escapes from the assylum and heads towards his target. after a long chase, he catches his enemy and beats him and mr. gibbons shows up and asks him to help him. max denies, so mr. gibbons team tranqualize him. max wakes up in a unknown place where his life is in danger. but he doesnt care if he is dead or alive. and mr. gibbons figures he has no interest in living. he is living only for one day in a year. if max is alive till that day.max wants revenge. so mr. gibbons makes a deal with him , that he will get his enemy on the same day every year. max agrees to the deal and now max has to work for gibbons.

max gets into the gun chamber of xxx. where all the guns and weapons are invented and placed. but max gets nothing but a contact lens which records what he sees, and technique to use any weapon after scanning from the lens. and also a pen which can show your gps location instead of location jammers even in water and space. so max enters the club in miami. max is a wanted man and every cop is looking for him for his actions. the bad guys recognizes max and asks him to join them. max agrees. max and the criminals head towards the sea in a boat. and there comes a submarine. and max enters the sub with them.

there was a big boss behind the escape of criminals, he gathered usefull criminals to threat the world. because he was old and tired of hidding. he needed freedom and in return he wont bomb places. max knows the places where they were bombing and where the bombs are located. when they come out of the sub. the criminals get a tip that the max is an agent. and the fights starts. max escapes from there mr. gibbons grabs him. the crimimal starts attcking mr. gibbons car in a humvee. and max gets rid of them.

after knowing the plan mr. gibbons starts realizing there is not much time to bring in the xxx for the battle. the bombing is gonna happen soon. the plan was to bomb miami from the waters of cuba. the criminals had their fighter jets and max heads towards the drop point of the criminals in a helicopter. max has to stop the bommbing

beacuse the bomber was a navy officer and his location was unknown. max has to figure his location. there is a big fight on the port of cuba and max gets the location of the navy officer. so max manages to fly the jet and reach at the launching point and saves the miami from getting bombed. and at the end gibbons offers him to ask anything which he want and max takes a fighter jet for himself and continues scewing the bad guys.
this story is for a frenchise

TWO

whats up with dave

dave is living in a studio apartment on rent. the landlord of the apartment is very annoying, greedy and always enters the room in stealth mode. dave is working in a online shopping company in a customer service dapartment. dave is a fat guy and always get bullied in the office. dave is called as mr. poop by his co worker and he is fed up of that. dave has a friend named eugene who sits next him in office. eugene wants dave to fight back to the bully's . dave never takes a stand for himself. dave likes a girl in office but he has no confidence to tell her, he has a fear of rejection and getting fired.dave is a looser in his own eyes and also the worlds.

dave has no social life. the only place he found peace was his apartment. one day the landlord of the apartment puts advertisement for a roommate online and orders dave to share the room with the new room mate. rocky watches the advertisement and applies for the bed in the appartment. so rocky is the dave's new room partner. rocky is a photographer by profession. rocky is always drunk and a womanizer. dave gets damm annoyed in the begining. but later he realizes rocky might help him to talk to the girl he likes. dave asks help from rocky and rocky starts teaching him some rules he made up.

dave becomes a party animal after teaming up with rocky. rocky discovers dave has a tallent of dancing. rocky starts posting his videos on facebook. dave becomes a sensation in the town. entire goa starts knowing dave for his moves. his life changes in the office. he is not a looser anymore. eugene also teams up with dave and rocky. they rock in every party in town. there are also many characters in the movie like the co ordinator, the reporter, the man on wheels and his wife, capatin underpants, the one legged dancer etc. the entire movies is completely a mad fun.

at the end dave's job gets in jeprody and he is also getting kicked out of the house because dave sends his nude dance video to the girl from the office. and the girl framed him to get fired. dave blames rocky for this rucus. dave and rocky fights with each other. but at the end rocky gets nude to save the dave's job and streams live marching the entire town with the help of his professional friends. rocky saves dave's job and they get back to their life with double the fun. this story is a adult comedy and recommende for children.

THREE

unlock

unlock is a online game. where there are two teams vipers and the panthers. they kill each other online. the cameras are all over the city and people who organized this game are very powerfull, the government is also a part of this game. the watchers are globally and they also bid on the team. the game is to unlock more points by reaching the location or kill the opponent. every point unlocked will have a benifit of travel and weapon. its the players choice to move to unlock the next point or head to kill their opponent. and each player can leave the game with money in millions after winning three rounds. once you enter you cannot exit the game. you have to be dead or you have to win three rounds. the players have a gajet attached to their chest which is unabe to remove the one who tries to remove a spike peirces into the heart from the gajet and their forearm also has a display giving information about the game and his opponent.

one new guy enters the game, though he didnt wanted to. his names is kevin. kevin is a bitchy guy. who is a youtuber. his real face is only known by the girls he dated. kevin is a parkour artist and good with jumping climbing and stufff like that. he always thugs the girls he dated and one day he has to pay for it. the organizer of unlock meets kevin in a party annd they offer him to play in the game. kevin denies and also insults the organizer. this puts the organizer on the edge and he drugs kevin in that party and as kevin wakes up he finds himself in the game. kevin's hands are locked and gajet on his chest. in the begining he doesnt understands whats happening but in time he understands his life is in danger. both the team panthers and the vipers are after him to kill.

kevin has no place to hide, he is surrounded with cameras and police is not helping him. he has to play the game and win. kevin unlocks his hands and unlocks few points he uses his skills to reach at his destination. there is a blood bath on the street. the game organizer kidnaps a girl who helped kevin during the game. and at the end kevin comes online and asks the watchers to find the unlock head quarters to save a girl. kevin is bitchy, a thug but he dont want a innocent to be dead. the watchers help kevin to reach and save the girl. kevin gets severly injured and gets in hospital.

when the unlock war is over kevin wakes up in the jail where he finds out that destroying the unlock headquarters didnt stop the game. the organizers are much more powerfull than he thought. so the round 2 begins.

this story is highly violent and recomended for children.

FOUR

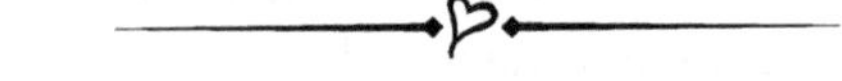

Time machine

This story is about a guy named egor. he is in his 40's. he is a science professor in a college. egor is always rude to everyone. egor always steals stuff fom the science lab. once egor stole some stuff and was about to get caught but he blames a student for the missing chemicals in the science lab.this puts students on the edge and they decides to keep a watch on the egor. they start following him. they watch egor is buying lots of gajets and stuffs from the junk yard and the chemical shops. the students start to supect that something is not right with this man. so one night the students sneak into his house.

when the student get into his house. they find that the egor is building something. the butler catches them and he explains the story behind the machine. the town is always suffered from storms and one night the storm took his wife and the child while they were travelling. and egor is making a time machine to go back in time and undo the travel during the storm.

the day came to start the time machine, which was being build by egor for years. the students watches egor from the key hole of his lab build in his house. the machine doesnt work and blasts and egor is in the machine and gets unconscious. egor meets his wife when he was unconsious. the wife explains that nothing was his fault, it was their time to go, you dont have to treat yourself and everyone badly. because their soul is alive in every living being. after this coversation with his wife he gets consious. egor watches the students have saved him.

now egor changes his way of living, he starts smilling at people and helping everyone. he also adopts homeless people andd keeps them safe during the storm. and he drives in storm towards his parents which he havent seen them for years. and the parents are praying in the storm and the door opens and the shadow of a man, woman and a child takes the amn away. and there is no explanation for the last shot.

FIVE

paristithi in english fatger's sacrifice

paristithi is a marathi drama. the strory is about a man named vithal. vithal was born in a poor family, his father dies when he was a child and his mother worked as a housekeeper in other peoples houses. vithal leaves his education and starts working small odd jobs.

when vithal grows up, vithal starts selling tickets outside the theatres which was a illegal thing. vithal got beat up by cops several times. what a man can do when he has no qualification. when ever vithal used to get beat up by cops. next day he used get himself in the hospital. the nuse and the vitahl had a connection. they get married. vithal stops the ticket selling job andr starts working in the factory like his father.

everything was back to normal, but the wife gets ill during her pregnancy and for extra money vithal starts selling the tickets again. vithal's mother bails him out by selling her last jewellery. as vithal comes out he watches that his mother is dead in the house and the wife is also dead in the hospital. vitthal is left with the child. vitthal makes a promise to his wife that before she dies that he will take care of his child and he will fullfil all his needs, and let him live his dreams, the child will never be unfortunate as they are. vitthal starts working harder.

vitthal worked in the factory and for extra money he also used to wash cars. this way years passed. vitthal never let the child down. vitthal satisfied all his needs and put him in a big reputed school. but the world is cruel. vithal's child vansh was bullied by other children that his father works as a car washer. vansh was embarressed of this siituation. vitthal knew this was the time when he had to act on this situation for the child because no one would offer him a reputed job due to his lack of education.

vitthal puts vansh in a reputed hostel outside the town, where no one could know what vitthal's occupation is. and his child will not be bullied. vansh grows up in the hostel and vitthal worked more harder in his job for his child. vitthal also lied to his child that he has started a business and everything is set. vitthal never brought his child to his town even in vacations to keep his job a secret. the son believed that his father is well settled which was a lie. this way more years passed. one day on the sons visit with the vitthal he talks about his dream. vansh wants to the pillot. and this is when more pain enters in vitthals life.

after meeting vansh vitthal comes back to his town and figures his son needs big number for the education of the pilot. so he sells his house to fullfills his sons dreams. vitthal knew that he can do nothing more than this. so he gives vansh the money for the education and acts as if he has done too much and he has to take care of his life now. vansh was in heart break because vitthal was not gonna meet him again as he spoke. and vitthal leaves from there.

vitthal was on the streets, he had nothing. he sold his house. he was fired from the factory because of poor hygiene. the only thing he had was his bucket and a peice of cloth which he used to wipe cars and earn money. but still he used to send money to his child. and this way many years passed.

once a female reporter was travelling in dark at night and she was being chased by the burglars. vitthal saved the girl. the girl called the police. the burglers ran from the sight of crime and police caught vitthal. as the reporter enters the police station she watches vitthal was arrested. she tells police to leave him immediatly. the reporter gets vitthal out of the police custody. she starts talking to him. vitthal tells her his life story.

after listening to his story, the reporter suggests vitthal that living this way is not the right way, vitthal should contact his son. vitthal denies meeting his son. vitthal explains to the reporter that if vansh comes to know the sacrifice that he has done. vansh will hate himself and vitthal doesnt want that. but still reporter keeps searching for vitthals son. at the end the reporter find vitthals son and informs about his father. the son and the father meet each other and the son takes his father away from the streets and takes him back to his home. and the reporter takes a picture of them going together . she reaches home and starts typing this wonderfull story and tittles it paristithi.

SIX

Paranoid

paranoid is a mental condition developes in the brain due to the events in the persons life. malcolm is a recovery man, who recovers money from people and delivers to the client which hired him. the job is not legit. malcolm makes a big number in this job. he has a partner too. unfortunately his partner dies in a accident . malcolm feels his partner was killed and he will be next untill he finds the killer. he gets paranoid.

malcolm doubts everyone, he thinks even his girlfriend can bring him death. he trusts no one and goes back in his past what all jobs he has done and who hired him. malcolm starts killing everyone of them, and before their death he asks the same question. why you want me dead. though the people he catched had no answers because no one is after him. malcolm still feels someone is out there to kill him. malcolm continues on this path of killing.

in the end malcolm gets shot by the police and lands up in the hospital. the officer who was working on the case informs him that the accident of his partner was just and accident. it was not an assasination. then malcolm realizes he killed all the people for no reason. but micheal escapes the hospital and gets into a ship and there he realizes that he has killed lots of people. and there will be people after him. and his paranoa continues even though he is leaving the country.

SEVEN

night out.

this story about three teen age girls alice, rachel and jane. they never went to any club or any disco in their life. when alice was a child, she had a childhood friend named tom. tom leaves goa and settles in mumbai with his parents. and after few years tom becomes a big film star. every year tom visits goa at 31st december for new years celebration. alice wants to meet tom by any means. she decides to find where tom celebrates his new year's eve and meet him. beacuse tom is a big superstar it i very difficut to find where he is clebrating his new years eve, so alice decides to search in every night club of goa to find tom. and thats where rachel and jane comes in the picture. they both joins alice to search tom.

alice, rachel and jane and were searching tom in every night club in goa. their life was in danger when they entered a chinese club. the chinese gangsters wanted to kidnap and rape them but a guy named frank saves their life and burns down the club. so the chinese gangsters are after frank and the girls for revenge. frank was librarian who lived with his grand mother. franks best friend charlie forces him to come with him in a night club. on the other hand a don was enjoying his time in the club but his partner wants him dead, so the partner hires an assasin to kill the don. in this situation a fight starts in the club and charlie gets arrested with a mad girl. frank was on his own with the girls.

alice does not let go and keeps searching for tom. frank knew the girls were in danger by the chinese gangsters. so frank joins them to help alice in her quest. there are more colourfull characters like the cop who talks like clint eastwood, a old man who is in love alice, david a funny charcter who is always in trouble. the entire night is an adventure.

finally alice meets tom in the morning. tom recognizes her and asks her to come with her in a private plane. but she denies because the night which gone through was most exciting night of her life. and the entire gang leaves the airport together.

this story is about a nights adventure.

EIGHT

mental

this story is about a mad man named mathew. mathew grew up with lot of love from his mother. his mother dies and when he grows up the world is not so good to him. mathew reeplies to people in his way, not by harming but doing horrible things to them. mathew has changed his nature due to this wolrd. mathew is still confused is the world crazy or he is. mathew behaves accentric all the time. mathew gets removed from various jobs due to his mischeif. but he has to survive for living and keeps on searching for jobs and at the end he gets fired.

the story is very funny. at the end mathew lands up in the mental assylum. the officer who puts him there thinks he will live rest of his life there. mathew remembers the words of his mom that " no one can stop you from being you or cage you for what you are. the world is equally yours like the everyone of them"

mathew escapes the mental assylum with more of the patients and the madness will be continued in the next part.

NINE

kombact

kombact is a game of illegal fights on a island. people who watch kombact are billionaires and bid on the fighters. kombact has inhouse fighters and participants from various regions. the winner is always from the kombact inhouse fighter the game i rigged. there is also a prize for the winners, gold worth in millions but till now no participant has won the gold. the game and the island is designed in such a way no one wins and escape. the fighters who participate land up dead.

kombact has no normal fights. the fighting arena always has lethal art effects. the fighters have to fight in steel cages, fire effects, quick sand, bridges, underwater etc. there are also animals in the fights like giant crocodiles. commodo dragons, gorilla, lions etc.

this time the participants are in the kombact for a purpose. zang wants revenge for his younger brother. drukken boxer johny cage thinks fighting is the only way out from prison. natasha enters the game to take revenge from her husband's killer, and when she is done she wants to escape the island which was impossible. natasha figured she is going to die in the island. so she keeps on convincing zang and drunken boxer named johny cage.

johny cage has a dark secret, he thinks that because of him his father and his coach died, johny should have been there for them. johny is been trained by a legend. johny has to drink alcohol to calm the demon inside him otherwise he may kill lots of people. the master of the kombact realizes johny can kill everyone in the kombact. so he offers him half the gold and leave. both zang and natasha forces him to take the prize and leave. johny exits the game. while he was going out of the island he figures no one escapes the kombact, zang and natasha will be dead soon. so he turns back to the island and fights the masters.

at the end after defeating all the fighters from the island. new kombact fighters enters the island. and the new fighters have special powers. and johny, zang and natasha are ready to fight their way out.

this story is highly violent and recomended for children.

TEN

finding

this story is about a man who is stuck in his past tragedy, he leaves his job and his family and settles in a new place. he avoids his family beacuse he is in lot of pain and his brain doesnt allows him to forget. when this man gets into his new place. he gets an letter at his house. and the letter has the information of abduction of a girl. the man feels alive for the first time.

the man leaves his country and reaches USA at the location and starts finding the girl. a taxi driver helps him. and he discovers how the human trafficking is taken place and how the people are delivered from every corner of the country.

the man kills the guy named howard smith who is invoolved in this horrible act of selling his daughter. and he meets everyone by the name of howard smith. but he gets caught by a social worker. everyone figures out. the man killed the howard smith for a reason. the human which were abducted were bought from a ship at a port called black point. its a big racket.

after reaching USA the man was in danger but he didnt let go, he kept on searching for the girl. a hooker on the street helps him and shows how things work. and he keeps on

finding the people behind the racket and where they keep them.
after researching the crazy man who was finding the girl finds out the truck driver who delivered the girls to the crime lord. the man also finds out that the truck driver is the sender of the letter. they all starts finding the girl. unfortunately the girl is been dead and left her child behind. the only proof to catch the crime lord is to save the baby and do the babies DNA test. because the girls which were marked were kept for the crime lord in a castle and the girl had a mark on her body.
many lives are lost to save the child, and at the end. the crime lord is caught and the baby is with the social worker. and the man declares his address in public and goes back to uk. even the goverment of UNITED KINGDOM supports him. after reaching his house he finds more letters. this means there are more people who are abducted and suppose to be found.
this story is violent and not recomended for children.

ELEVEN

Drunk detective

the story is about ex cop who is a working as a detctive. in the first episode the case is about a cannibal living in the society. the cannibals victims are mostly woman. he removes the internal organs of the woman. the police solving the case feels as they are facing some man who is killing and dealing with the human organs. the cop working on the case takes help from the detective. but detctive figures the crime is not as it looks like. the suspect was very difficult to catch. detective finds the cannibal by tracing his moves and by understanding his method of killing victims.

the second episode is about the blackmagic. the abduction of children and their body found in various location with a satanic mark on the victims body. the entire police force is unable to find the guy. but the detctive figures out the pattern of the crime and catches the supects. and even saves the last victim.

The third episode is about a public bully comes back with a vengeance. the killings of the colledge student is mystery in town. and the detctive catches the suspect by tracking the crimes of the dead ones. as everyone gets surprised that the killer is from the family of the victim who was bullied by the dead college student.

The 4th episode is about the serial killer. whose victims are only cops. the friend of detctive gets shot in this episode and detcetive finds the suspects. but the guys were dead before the cops catches them. detective goes in jail to find out the reason behind those killings and who are the killers attached with. detecetive discovers a big chain of the killers but he has nothing to prove than rott in jail.

In the fifth episode detective is bailed. this crime is severe of all its about a snuff porn. girls are filmed while they are raped and killed. first they are abducted by a unknown cab driver and then they are drugged and taken to the pig farm. in the scary pig farm they are killed with knife and swords and filmed. it was very difficult to make out its a studio or a original farm. but detective finds the killer and brings back the girl he was appointed for.

the sixth episode is about the past of the detective and the human trafficking in a big number. and the people are forced to test medicines and chemicals on their body. it was a big medical racket. detective uncovers this dangerous people and saves lots of lives. but at the end the detctive gets severly injured and dies.

this story is highly violent and not recomended for children.

TWELVE

Cannibal

This story is about a colledge group, who are champing in woods, and they come accross the evil man eaters. they kill the colledge group one by one and the struggle to survive from the man eaters becomes impossible. but the group somehow manges to outrun the jungle and reach the way back home.
this story is adult and highly violent. not recomended for children.

THIRTEEN

Artist

this story is about an killer artist. artist is killing people in his way. he diguise himself and kills his opponent one by one. its a case of vendetta. he is killing people who are probably bad and threat to him and his family. his enemies are basically bad people. the thing is no one knows his real name and how he looks. he is always disguised. he is an true artist, he knows how to make portrait, act and sing. and beside that he can change his face to anyone using make up. he is highly skilled artist and a trained killer.

the girl he married is his childhood friend. she understands him. he is not a bad guy. he just cant things let go. they travel various places in diguise to live a normal life. but artist always finds a way to make enemies. so as the artist takes his revenge. they just leave the town and settle somewhere else. with a fake name and fake id. he is a good document forger too.

this time artist gets into a fight with the 5 partners. they are with high contact and lots of power. they kind of own the town. they burn down the artists house andd artist manages to escape from the fire with his wife. artist settles down in next town but the incident keeps on revolving in his head. artist leaves his family and heads for revenge after a long research about five partners. he starts killing them one by one. this is when a detective comees in the picture. detective follows his footsteps and finds his family. detective meets his wife. the wife explains the detective about the crimes of 5 partners. artist kills everyone of them except the 5th. no one has any clue who is he. but artist uncovers this mystery. the 5th partner is the comissioner who has hired the detecetive to catch the artist.

at the end artist wins the battle with the 5 partners. but his name is still a mystery. and he is out living a life with his wife without a vengeance and no more mask as he promissed his wife. and the world is still unknown what the artist looks like and who is he.

FOURTEEN

Afterlife

this story about a guy named mark, he is a virgin in his 40's. he is a virgin. he is been cheated by his best friend. mark's only sin is that he has jerkked off watching porn and kissed a married woman. mark dies in a accident. and this is how the story begins.

when mark dies his soul enters the gate of jugement. mark's deeds will be calculated at the gate of judgement in a cradle. depending on the mark's deed he will be sended to hell or heaven. mark has no good deeds in his life. so gets thrown in the hell. mark still doeesnt knows he is dead yet. after spending more time he realizes he is dead. mark is a joke hell. beacuse there are hardcore sinners and he came in hell only for kiss and jerking off.

marks meets devil, devil had a soft corner for him because he didnt harm anyone. mark becomes friends with the devil. devil shows him the punishments and sinners after they die. devil realizes his only sin is that he has jerrked off. devil feels that mark doesnt deserves to be in hell. devil doesnt wants him there, he wants to tranfer mark's soul in heaven . but he cannot do anything. because its never his choice to put the soul. its the individuals deeds decides where he will land up. hell or heaven.

so devil meets the sineater. who has the way to send him to heaven. but the sineater has a appetite, he can only consume sin if his belly is full. but the sin eater can only consume the big sin like murder. devil decides if mark keeps on sinning he may reach at the level of murder. now mark has to sin more. so devil decides to send him back to earth and allow him to enter bodies and sin so he can fullfill sineaters appetite. mark gies back to earth and starts sinning. there are several funny moments. mark often meets a woman soul on earth and she always asks him to help her. but mark was busy sinning

mark used to get in other peoples body and do sex to their partners. mark was almost to reach at sineaters appetite. mark enters a body to sin. and as mark comes out of the body after sex. the man kills the girla and starts robbing her house. mark gets disturebd watching this. mark cannot hurt him beacuse he can only enter the body if te man is horny. the story turns sad. mark meets the ghost of the lady and helps her saving her sister and at the end mark returns back by doing a good deed. automatically he is transferred to heaven. and mark discovers in heaven that the god and the devil is the same. and he learns humans decide where they willl land up.

this story is completely imagenary. there are adult scenes but this story teaches us keep doing the good. your deeds are been calculated and if you do bad you will suffer. this story also shows the punishment in the hell for sinners.

this story is a n adult comedy and not recomended for children.

FIFTEEN

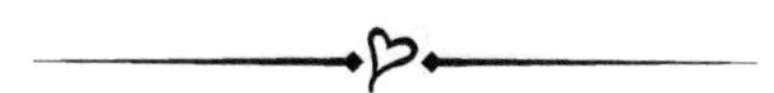

Affair

A unique story about nymphomania and satryasis, a mental condition not known by many people. many secrets will be opened which is unknown by the people. and how a struggle of a business makes you do go down. this script also includes the social network habitatants of the generation. its a highly educated film.
The character in the story is rocky, movie also shows how he changes and turns into a monster. there are also conducts like blackmail, adultry, fighting in clubs and street hawk. the tittle of the movie is affair and the secret behind the tittle will be opened shortly.
this story has highly adult content and not rcomended for children

SIXTEEN

Streets

streets is the prequel of the story affair, this story is about rocky and how he gets into drugs. this story is about whenn there were no androids, no high class celular phone and no discipline in the streets of mumbai. this story is about gang who does lots gangbang on the street and the reality of the nights. the contents are highly abussive and disturbing.
the story also shows the different effects of drugs on the generation and their ups and down. the world aint no sunshine, its very nasty and mean place. there are deaths from overdose. robbery for the yeyos. and the lust to comqueer their needs. the story is also about rocky and his gang, what they conqueer and how they fall down. drugs are very bad thing. it makes a man inhuman, becarefull for what you wish for. at the end the flow will never let you be for what you are.

9 798887 171999

Printed by Libri Plureos GmbH in Hamburg, Germany